JIMMY ZEST, SUPER PEST

Jimmy Zest is such trouble. He just can't seem to learn that his plans never work out. That doesn't make him give up on them, though, which is something that annoys his friends. Mind you, they still join in as pesky Zesty causes chaos in a castle, tries to scrounge some scones and cooks up a crazy competition in someone else's kitchen.

JIMMY ZEST, SUPER PEST

Sam McBratney

Illustrated by Tim Archbold

GALAXY

This edition first published in
Great Britain 2002
by
Macmillan Children's Books
This Large Print edition published by
BBC Audiobooks Ltd
by arrangement with
Macmillan
2004

ISBN 0 7540 7888 4

First published in 1989 as *Zesty Goes
Cooking* by Hamish Hamilton
Children's Books
'Lovehearts and Dungeons' and
'Goodbye, Miss Quick' first published
1982 by Hamish Hamilton Children's
Books in *Zesty*.

McBratney, Sam
  Jimmy Zest, super pest.—Large print ed.
  1. Zest, Jimmy (Fictitious character)—Juvenile fiction
  2. Inventors—Juvenile fiction 3. Children's stories, English
  4. Large type books
  I. Title II. Archbold, Tim III. McBratney, Sam. Zesty goes
  cooking
  823. 9'14[J]

ISBN 0-7540-7888-4

Printed and bound in Great Britain by
Antony Rowe Ltd., Chippenham, Wiltshire

CONTENTS

1	Lovehearts and Dungeons	1
2	Scone Wars	39
3	Egg-splosions!	57
4	Goodbye, Miss Quick	89

CHAPTER ONE

LOVEHEARTS AND DUNGEONS

The last lesson of the day was History.

Most of the pupils in Miss Quick's class were dying to get started because their new project required lots of cutting out and sticking in. Nothing could put life into History quite like scissors and glue.

They were about to make a copy of the famous Bayeux Tapestry on clean, white sheets of paper. When they finished it—so Miss Quick had promised—it would go on display in the corridor for the whole school to look at.

Miss Quick divided them into pairs and gave each pair a picture of the tapestry. Shorty, whose real name was Noel Alexander, examined his picture carefully, and frowned.

'Miss,' he said, 'those Normans couldn't draw the pension.'

'Why is that, Noel?'

'Look, Miss. They've got two horses in a ship the size of a canoe and their soldiers are as skinny as matchsticks. That's no way to draw.'

Confident that *he* could do as good a job as the ladies who had made the real tapestry, Shorty reached for a clean, white sheet.

The room became a hive of activity. Colouring pencils rattled on tabletops, scissors sliced through paper, rubbers and sharpeners were thrown from one row to the next. A sound like the hammer of a woodpecker's beak turned out to be Shorty putting dots all over his Normans.

Then Miss Quick noticed that two lazy people hadn't even started yet.

'Nicholas? Why are you holding Stephen Armstrong's wrist?'

This was a very difficult question to know how to answer. Knuckles, also known as Nicholas Alexander, had been using the face of Legweak's watch to reflect a tiny circle of light on to the ceiling. By turning Legweak's wrist he made it dart about like a lively little mouse. The two boys had watched the moving light for so long that they had practically hypnotized themselves.

Legweak slapped a hand over the face of his watch, but of course he was too late.

'You two boys can't sit together, especially when there's glue about. Nicholas, come up here—you will sit at Mandy's table and work with her.'

'Aw, Miss.'

'Move!'

Mandy Taylor, who had been hunched over her work, straightened her back in dismay.

'But, Miss. Penny and me . . .'

'It will be quite all right, Mandy, Nicholas is going to be good. Move over.'

She moved over. Mandy moved over as far as she possibly could, but still only a small space separated her from her new partner. As Knuckles sat down, Shorty gave a low wolf whistle and Gowso giggled like a fool to see a boy and a girl working together. If looks could kill, Mandy would have murdered Shorty and Gowso there and then.

Before long Mandy decided that she needed to borrow some glue from Penny's table at the back of the room.

'It's desperate!' she whispered quickly. 'He's colouring the horses in *green*.' And she hurried back to her seat.

Just before home time, Miss Quick amazed them all with an announcement.

'By the way, I'm taking you on a school trip next Friday. We're going to see a real Norman castle with walls and dungeons and things—the view from the keep is absolutely marvellous, so I'm told.'

At the front of the room Knuckles stopped sharpening Mandy Taylor's new colouring pencils. He loved History with scissors and glue. He loved History when it was colouring in. But the best History of all was History with deep, dark dungeons. The others were just as enthusiastic, for a school trip was the next best thing to a day off. Of course you had to do some work, but still. Shorty was delighted.

'Oh, Miss. Fantastic.'

Jimmy Zest raised an arm very straight, and Miss Quick sighed as if she knew that something was coming.

'Miss, has this castle we're going to got machicolations?'

'Has it got what?'

'Machicolations?'

'I dare say it has, Jimmy Zest, we'll find out when we get there. Have a look at this, everyone.'

She held up a board with a metal clip at the top. 'You must each have one of these to lean on. The clip stops your pages blowing away, and that's important. If you haven't got a clipboard, get one. And bring a proper lunch, you can't do a day's work on yogurt. And remember, this castle has lots of dangerous places so there will be no tomfoolery when we get there. Tidy up your tables, please, the bell will be going soon.'

*　　　*　　　*

Gowso, Penny Brown, Jimmy Zest and Mandy Taylor walked home from school together and, naturally enough, they talked quite a lot about the school trip to the Norman castle. Jimmy Zest tried to have a conversation about machicolations but the others didn't know what they were.

'I wonder,' said Penny Brown, 'if Miss Quick is a good driver. Suppose we crash and she wrecks the school minibus. Flute!'

The topic of the school trip lasted them very well until they reached the shops, where they met Legweak.

He had some fascinating news for Mandy Taylor. 'There's something written about you on the back of the telephone box,' he said.

They raced over to have a look. On the back of the telephone box outside Mrs Worthington's sweetie shop, some joker had chalked an enormous white loveheart with this extraordinary statement in the middle of it:

They all stood as if their tongues had been taken prisoners. Then Penny Brown spoke at last. 'That is a scandal, you know.'

Knuckles wasn't with them, so no one knew what he thought about this piece of slander. There could be no doubt, however, that Mandy Taylor did not find it amusing. Calmly she turned to Gowso, who happened to be grinning. 'Do you see something funny, Philip McGowan?'

The cold in her voice withered the smile on Gowso's face. Mandy borrowed a tissue from Penny Brown and, with three or four powerful strokes, removed the offensive scribble from the public eye.

Then she and Penny continued up the road with their heads so close together that they appeared to have been joined.

Jimmy Zest bought a packet of wine gums in Worthington's. Gowso and Legweak gathered round him like vultures.

*   *   *

The following day during break, Jimmy Zest hammered on his table until they all paid attention. Then he shouted out, 'Roll up, roll up, get 'em here, just what you need at a special price, roll up.'

'Roll yourself up, Zesty,' said Penny Brown.

She saw what was coming—some diabolical scheme to separate innocent people from their money. But, as usual, curiosity got the better of Shorty.

'What are you selling, Zesty?'

'A whole lot of what nobody needs,' called Penny Brown.

But she was wrong. Jimmy Zest produced three stiff clipboards—just the very thing for taking with you on a school trip to a windy place. He had made them the previous evening from a piece of his dad's hardboard.

Gowso didn't have a clipboard, yet.

'What's your price, Zesty?' he asked.

'Only fifty pence per board.'

'Huh, you could make your own board cheaper, Gowso.'

Jimmy Zest turned to face the heckling Penny Brown.

'Wrong again, Penelope. The metal clips alone cost more than that in the shops. OK?' He failed to add that he hadn't actually bought the clips himself, and that every penny of the money was clear profit.

Gowso and Legweak snapped up a board each.

'Would you like to buy the third board, Penelope?' Jimmy Zest politely asked.

Penny Brown slipped a hand under her table and pulled out her own board. Her intention had been to demonstrate to the snook that he was not the only one who could manufacture clipboards—but something changed her mind.

These words, inside a loveheart, had been chalked on her board in large print:

Knuckles
loves
Amanda (VERY TRUE)

Some of the boys began to smile.

'Who is doing this? I'd like to know,' asked Mandy Taylor grimly.

Of course they all looked equally surprised and innocent. Shorty said, 'Definitely not me', and Gowso repeated like an echo, 'Definitely not me'. Jimmy Zest shook his head when Penny Brown accused him with a silent glare and Legweak said, 'Nope'.

As for Knuckles, he didn't seem to mind at all that some secret sneak was making accusations about him but he did lean over and wipe out the words VERY TRUE.

Up in the air went Mandy Taylor's finger, which she wielded as though it had become a dangerous weapon.

'Well it didn't write itself. It's against the law to write lies about people and if I get the person responsible, he'll really be for it, I'm warning you.'

For the rest of the day Mandy could not concentrate. She couldn't help thinking about those lovehearts. One of the boys had to be drawing them. If only she knew which one.

*   *   *

Friday morning arrived.

As Miss Quick's pupils checked through their equipment in the classroom they looked as though they might be setting out on an expedition to some faraway country. Anoraks and mats lay about everywhere, and the tables were littered with lunch boxes and clipboards and flasks with hot liquids inside them.

Legweak opened Gowso's flask and a rush of escaping steam shot up his nose.

'Gowso's got hot chocolate!' he announced. Miss Quick, in her coat, handed out sheets with diagrams and questions.

'Miss,' shouted Gowso, 'can Mandy Taylor sit beside Knuckles in the bus?'

'Grow up, Gowso,' Penny Brown advised him.

At the far side of the room Miss Quick picked up Knuckles's clipboard. It was enormous—twice the size of anybody else's. Also, it looked as though it had been gnawed by sharp teeth.

'Where did you get this?'

'It's the roof of my guinea pig hutch, Miss.'

'Show me your clip.'

When Knuckles produced a yellow plastic clothes peg, Penny Brown could only gasp. What would members of the public think when they saw a pupil walking round an ancient monument carrying the lid of his guinea pig hutch and a yellow clothes peg? Shorty had a clothes peg, too. His was lime green.

But Miss Quick was the one who mattered, and she didn't seem to mind

12

about the school's good name. Quietly she said that they had better get a move on. 'And remember to *walk* in the corridor.'

Five minutes later they were on their way.

In the main building of the school, jealous heads turned towards the window to watch the minibus passing through the gates.

'Look at all the suckers working,' Knuckles shouted out. 'Bye-bye, school.'

According to Legweak, Miss Quick drove like a snail. Even so, they had a pleasant journey, especially when Knuckles discovered a packet of fruit drops in Gowso's pocket. Shorty sat the whole time with a lime-green clothes peg on his nose and only took it off when the minibus lurched to a halt on the gravel surface of the castle car park.

The Norman castle occupied a commanding position at the summit of a steep hill. Although the castle walls were partially hidden for the moment behind a clump of mature trees, the visitors had a clear view of the forbidding keep and battlements against a background of shifting clouds. Jimmy Zest screwed up his eyes to see whether it had machicolations.

'Miss, can you pretend you're William the Conqueror?' Knuckles asked.

'Nicholas, dear, be whoever you like—only be good.'

Pencils and clipboards appeared, and they began to get their work done. Shorty stayed at Jimmy Zest's elbow to scrounge good answers. Question number four on the sheet gave him some difficulty, because you had to draw something interesting. He picked the chapel. It was in ruins already and Shorty figured that his drawing couldn't make it look any worse.

Then Miss Quick led them up the triangular stone steps of the spiral staircase, round and round and round, all the way to the top of the keep. Legweak said it was like climbing up a corkscrew, and Miss Quick giggled.

'Oh dear,' she said. 'I'm out of breath.'

'It looks like you're getting old, Miss,' Shorty said gravely.

Penny Brown and Mandy Taylor discovered a little square room out of the wind. They saw from their diagrams that it might have been a lady's bedroom in Norman times. Through a little slit window in the wall there was a lovely view down the long valley where, once upon a time, the Norman lords had ridden out in helmets and armour like people from the Bayeux Tapestry, but the girls didn't see the view.

They saw something else. Above the window they saw a twentieth-century loveheart.

Mandy Taylor
loves
William the Conqueror
(true)

'I'll bet you that's Nicholas Alexander!' shouted Penny Brown.

Such a sight would have sunk the

patience of
a saint,
never
mind an
ordinary
sinner like
Mandy
Taylor.
She kicked
the wall
with her
foot, and
hurt her
toes enough to
make her calm down.

'Why do you think it's him?' she said.

'It must be. Who else is going round the castle calling himself William the Conqueror? He couldn't conquer a stick insect! Before this day is out, we'll get him.'

Mandy was much more doubtful. In her opinion, Knuckles Alexander was almost invincible.

'How?'

'I don't know yet, but we'll think of something.'

At that moment Legweak put his head round the door.

'You two have to hurry up.'

'What for, Legweak?'

'Miss Quick says we're going down to the dungeons!'

*   *   *

Jimmy Zest had thought to bring a torch with him, so Miss Quick allowed him to lead the way down through the spooky tunnel—which was dark, and deep, and very cold. However, neither the dark nor the chill of the ancient stones could quieten the pupils of Miss Quick's class:

'Walk on your own heels, Knuckles.'

'I'm not near your heels.'

'WAAAAH!'

'You're not much of a ghost, Gowso.'

'Hard luck,' said the ghost, 'my name's not Gowso.'

After seventy-five steps—Jimmy Zest was counting—Miss Quick unexpectedly switched on a light. Some people objected that this was cheating a bit, but Legweak wasn't one of them.

17

A sensation of being buried alive came over him so powerfully that Miss Quick sent him out of the dungeons immediately.

'It's claustrophobia,' she explained to the others, 'he doesn't like to be closed up in confined places.'

'My aunty's got that,' Shorty said.

They were hemmed in on all sides by the circular walls of a domed chamber. At intervals round the walls there were dark recesses where the light could not penetrate.

'If these walls could speak,' Miss Quick whispered, 'I wonder what they would say?'

'Quite a lot, Miss,' Shorty whispered back.

It was Knuckles who noticed the arch-shaped door at the far end of this, the main dungeon. As the others gathered eagerly round him, he slid back the heavy bolt and swung the door open—it creaked horribly—to reveal a pitch-black hole.

Was there anything in there—the skeleton, maybe, of an ancient Saxon? Knuckles, who was very proud of his discovery, said, 'Miss, I'll go in and have a look.' But Miss Quick decided that they had seen enough down here.

'Shut the door, Nicholas. Everybody write down what you think of this place, then we'll go back to the minibus for some lunch.'

Penny Brown wrote that the people who came down here in the olden days probably never saw the sun again. And then suddenly, mysteriously, an idea came into her head. She thought that in there, behind that heavy old door, was the perfect place to teach a certain person a real lesson—one that he would never forget.

Could she and Mandy snare him in the dungeon?

After lunch, Miss Quick announced to her class that they could go exploring on their own, provided that they promised to stay off the battlements.

This would be good for them, she thought. Also, it would allow her to drink her coffee in peace. She had just picked up her flask when she heard a wild and frightful scream coming from the chapel ruins.

'Oh my stars!' she declared. 'Those twins, I'll murder them.'

One glance through the crumbling chapel walls told all. A scene worthy of the Bayeux Tapestry unfolded before her eyes as Stephen Armstrong slid down a gravestone with his tongue hanging out and his eyeballs rolling, evidently quitting the world. The reason for this drama became apparent when Philip McGowan and Noel Alexander rushed forward in triumph, shouting, 'Got you, Legweak.'

'You're dead, Legweak.'

'I know, I know I'm dead,' said the victim. 'Do you think I'm stupid?'

Legweak sat up smartly enough when he saw Miss Quick climbing over a low part of the chapel wall. Shorty launched himself into an explanation.

'We're playing Normans, Miss. It's Gowso and me against William the Conqueror and Legweak. We got Legweak with two arrows—zip, zip!'

'So I see. Listen, boys, if you must die, please do it quietly.'

'Fair enough, Miss. Miss, will you

make sure Legweak doesn't move while we get after Knuckles?'

'I will do no such thing,' said Miss Quick.

Like a warning, the highest notes of Legweak's dying agony had carried to the great hall of the keep, where William the Conqueror himself had taken refuge in a stone chimney.

It was two against one, now. Knuckles gripped the roof of his guinea pig hutch tightly, like a shield, and adjusted the hat on his head. It was a Samurai warrior origami hat. Zesty had made it for him out of a lunch wrapper, especially for this battle.

A sound near the spiral staircase made him totally alert. Quietly he raised his bow, ready to THUNK an arrow into whoever was coming.

It was Penny Brown with an urgent message. 'They shot Legweak. Shorty's in the dungeon. *Hurry*, Knuckles.'

Then she was gone, he heard her feet rattling on the staircase far below.

Penny Brown, feet flying, and with her heart beating in her throat, skipped down the last flight of steps into the dungeon, where Mandy was waiting for her.

'Is he coming?'

'I don't know!'

'Oh, are we *wise*?' cried the doubting Mandy Taylor as they hid.

It was too late now for doubts. Nicholas Alexander was descending cautiously into their trap. Soon they saw the grotesque and moving shadow of his ridiculous origami hat on the curve of the dungeon wall. He did not fail to notice that the door of the small dungeon lay open like an invitation. Mandy gripped Penny's wrist so hard that Penny hit her a dig in the ribs with her elbow.

When Knuckles crawled in, Penny Brown left her hiding place as if she had been shot from a bow, slammed the door shut—and rammed the bolt home.

'Got you!' she said.

The voice from the other side of the door—the dark, shut-in side of the door—sounded muffled.

'You're a sly one. You're working for Shorty.'

'We're not working for Shorty. We'll let you out, Nicholas Alexander, if you promise not to write any more lies about Mandy on walls and things and if you don't promise, you'll stay in there until everything rots but your bones.'

'What are you talking about? I didn't write anything.'

'You did so. You wrote she loves William the Conqueror, didn't he, Mandy?'

Mandy Taylor tried to make this sound like just a normal, friendly game.

'Please, Knuckles, just say you won't write any more about me and we'll let you out.'

It didn't work.

'It's not my fault if you love William the Conqueror.'

'Right! Then stay there,' said Mandy, who had heard exactly what it took to stiffen her resolve. 'There are laws against people like you. Let's go, Penny.'

They didn't actually go just yet, for Penny Brown remembered how Legweak couldn't bear to be shut up in dark places.

23

'Maybe,' whispered Penny, 'he's got claus...'

'Claustrophobia,' said Mandy, whose vocabulary was excellent.

So they waited, listening, in case Knuckles panicked and began to yell and hammer on the door like a mad thing.

Nothing of the sort happened. The muffled voice began to sing. It sang roughly to the tune of 'John Brown's Body':

'Mandy Taylor loves William the Conqueror,

Mandy Taylor loves William the Conqueror,

Mandy Taylor loves William the Conqueror,

And so does Penny Brown.'

'You will *never* get out of there,' yelled Penny Brown.

They left him still singing, with their consciences clear.

*   *   *

In the courtyard in front of the castle keep, Miss Quick was unaware of these events happening far below her feet. Their time here had almost come to an end and she had her camera in her hand.

'Practise your smile, Noel. Has anybody seen Jimmy Zest or is he still sketching machicolations? Penny and Mandy, over here girls. Stand at the door of the keep, and *smile* everybody, please.'

'Miss,' Shorty pointed out, 'if you take a photo of Mandy Taylor you'll need a new camera.'

Miss Quick took the risk. After snapping the group, she turned the camera on the castle. Shorty watched her for a while, then asked a worrying question.

'Miss, where's Knuckles? We haven't seen him for ages?'

A little furrow of concern appeared on Miss Quick's brow. Nicholas Alexander was the very boy she liked to keep an eye on.

'Has anyone seen Nicholas recently?' she called out.

Penny Brown and Mandy Taylor, who knew exactly where Nicholas was, were worried too. They began to wonder what would happen if Miss Quick found him shut away in the dungeon like a forgotten prisoner. Probably she would regard it as dangerous tomfoolery and they would get into trouble and Nicholas Alexander would love it.

Quickly they raced down the twisting steps to the level of the last dungeon, where the electric light still burned.

'He's stopped singing,' Mandy said breathlessly.

Penny Brown pulled back the bolt.

'We think you've been taught a lesson,' she said into the pitch-black hole. 'You can come out now.'

Nothing stirred in the dungeon. Was he in there at all? Penny wanted to put her head in for a look but she was afraid of a hand grabbing her.

'Could someone have let him out?' whispered Mandy.

A voice spoke.

'Nobody let me out. I'm still here.'

Penny Brown heard the creak of a gate at the top of the steps.

'Come out of there this minute, Nicholas Alexander, Miss Quick is looking for you all over the place.'

'I can't come, can I? I'm a prisoner. Somebody locked me in this dungeon.'

His evil plan suddenly became transparently clear. He would stay in there deliberately and so cause trouble for the girls by disgracing them.

'It was only a joke,' Mandy said uneasily. 'Can't you even take a joke, for goodness' sake?'

'It wasn't a joke. You two shut me in here because she loves William the

27

Conqueror.'

Mandy Taylor yelled so loudly that her throat hurt, 'I DO NOT LOVE WILLIAM THE CONQUEROR, YOU ROTTEN EVIL SCHEMER.' And this was the moment when Miss Quick stepped into the dungeon.

She was still wearing that frown. First she looked at the girls and then at the open dungeon door.

'Well, Mandy, I'm glad to hear that you do not love William the Conqueror. It's probably just as well since he has been dead for over nine hundred years. What is this? Who is in that small dungeon?'

Mandy Taylor was affronted. She could only stand there twisting the ring on her little finger as she realized that any moment now, the truth would come out. Nicholas Alexander was bound to squeal on them and Miss Quick would see how she and Penny were guilty of dangerous tomfoolery, but the worst thing was—she would have to tell about those embarrassing lovehearts!

Miss Quick switched on Jimmy

Zest's torch and knelt down. Her knees snapped like dry twigs. The beam of the torch lit up the dark hole and there he was, sitting on his hunkers in an origami hat. The light from the torch also showed that he had a clothes peg dangling from his left ear lobe.

'It's only me, Miss.'

The sight of him made Miss Quick slowly shake her head.

'You were determined to get in there, weren't you? Come out, we thought you were lost.' Knuckles crawled out and dusted himself down with his palms.

'We were pretending to be Normans, Miss. I'm William the Conqueror.'

'In that hat?'

And Miss Quick studied Knuckles in a thoughtful way, as if to wonder for a moment how History would have turned out if William the Conqueror had been anything like Nicholas Alexander.

Eventually she said, 'Well, the pretending is over, we have to go home. Did you have a good day?'

'Miss,' said Knuckles with feeling, 'it

was fantastic.'

'Good. Penny, switch out the light for me please and we'll leave the poor Normans in peace.'

'Yes, Miss Quick,' said Penny Brown.

She was relieved—and so was Mandy Taylor—to have got out of that so lightly.

'Penny,' Mandy Taylor said quietly as they came up the dungeon steps, 'I think maybe he didn't do it. Maybe he is innocent.'

'Why?'

'I don't know, I've just got that feeling. I'm nearly sure it was somebody else. Maybe Legweak.'

Mandy Taylor had another feeling as she emerged from the dungeons into the light of day—that she hadn't yet seen the last of those despicable lovehearts.

*   *   *

Back at the minibus, people gathered up their belongings for the journey home. Gowso drank the last dribble of his cold chocolate and Shorty asked

Miss Quick for his answer sheet so that he could write down the word MACHICOLATIONS before he forgot it. Miss Quick looked as though wonders would never cease, and ordered them all into their seats.

Knuckles pinched Shorty's clothes peg and wore it on his other ear all the way home.

By the time they arrived back at school, even Mr Jones the patrolman had locked up his big lollipop and quit the premises, but nobody complained about the lateness of the hour. Mandy Taylor thanked Miss Quick very much for a lovely day. Then they gathered up their anoraks and macs and clipboards and flasks and their various souvenirs and went home.

As Miss Quick was about to climb into the minibus in order to park it, something near to the bottom of the door caught her eye and made her pause.

A finger had been busy. The loveheart in the dust said:

Mandy Taylor
loves
Knuckles
(True XXOOXOO)

'Somehow I doubt that,' she said to herself. 'I'll see to that cheeky imp on Monday. If I remember.'

*   *   *

Those dreaded Monday mornings almost always started in the same old way—with English and Maths. Miss Quick liked to double-dose them after the weekend, when they were fresh.

However, this Monday was different. The gluepots appeared. The scissors were counted out. Colouring pencils clattered on the tabletops again, and they worked for a solid hour to finish their Bayeux Tapestry for the corridor wall.

Mandy Taylor's section of the tapestry was called The Battle, that is to say, the Battle of Hastings. It was full of wounded soldiers, stricken horses and flying arrows. As a matter of fact, Mandy was quite pleased with the work of her partner, Knuckles. True, he had given the Normans green horses, and he had made the wounded Saxons bleed all over the page by using a red felt tip: but all that colour made their bit of the tapestry look very bright indeed. Miss Quick looked at it and said, 'Hmm.'

Then she announced that the time had come for the grand pinning up of the tapestry.

'Mandy, Penny, Nicholas and Jimmy Zest, you will be the stickers-up in the corridor. Take scissors and sticky tape outside with you. The rest of the class will read library books until you call them out with their piece of the tapestry. Make sure that you get the pieces in the right order, and when you have finished, we will all go out and have a look.'

This method worked very well, for a while. Gowso, sitting by the window, had a good view of what was happening in the corridor, and the Bayeux Tapestry began to look very impressive indeed as each piece of the story of the

Norman invasion was fitted into its proper place.

Jimmy Zest came to the door of the classroom.

'Miss, we're ready for Shorty's piece.'

'Noel—out you go.'

Less than two minutes later, Gowso stood up and peered goggle-eyed into the corridor. 'Miss, Miss, there's a fight out there!'

A fight! Legweak jumped up on his seat and the rest of the class all stood up and looked outside, for the sound of raised voices could clearly be heard in the corridor.

'Sit down!' roared Miss Quick, especially at Legweak. 'Every single one of you, stay where you are!'

Nobody budged, for the rays coming from Miss Quick's eyes would have fried eggs.

Then Miss Quick raced into the corridor to see for herself what was happening.

Jimmy Zest stood to one side, pretending to be invisible. Penny Brown had evidently forgotten that she was in school to judge by the tone of

34

her voice as she shouted, 'You rotten snook you, Shorty,' and Mandy Taylor, quite livid, had her fists clenched at her side. Noel Alexander stared at the sheet in his hand. His contribution to the Bayeux Tapestry had been ripped in two.

At last they saw the teacher, and calmed down. Miss Quick allowed them a moment or two to compose themselves, then turned to the reliable Jimmy Zest for information.

'Tell me what happened here. Hurry up.'

Jimmy Zest had no choice.

'It's Shorty's bit of tapestry, Miss.'

'What about it?'

'We're not putting it up, that's what about it,' said Nicholas Alexander bluntly. 'He's ruined all our good work about the Normans.'

The astonished Miss Quick seized the evidence out of Noel Alexander's hands. She could see nothing wrong with it, except that it was in two bits. Then her eyes spotted the mischief.

'Oh,' she said. 'I see. Now I see.'

He had drawn a row of Normans sitting in a boat. Each Norman had a shield—the shields hung over the side of the boat. Each shield had been drawn in the shape of a heart. And in the middle of each heart, in tiny capital letters, it said, M T L N A.

Miss Quick shifted her gaze from the torn page and fixed it on Shorty, who looked very sorry that the Bayeux Tapestry had ever been stitched.

'You also wrote on the school minibus, didn't you, Noel?'

'And my clipboard, Miss.'

'And the Norman castle. And the telephone box up the road.'

'Miss,' said Shorty, 'I could wash the minibus for you.'

'You will not wash the minibus. I suppose you think that sort of thing is amusing?'

'Not any more, Miss.'

'Why did you do it, then?'

'Well, you see, they were sitting beside each other. I did it for a laugh.'

'Nobody's laughing, nobody thinks it's funny to have their project spoiled, even your brother has told you so. Go inside, all of you. I'll have more to say about this.'

There were not many minutes left before break. Nobody dared speak in Miss Quick's class, for there was Trouble in the air.

Miss Quick made a short announcement. She said that Noel Alexander would remain behind during break to begin his section of the tapestry all over again.

'Also, Noel, you have an apology to make unless I am very much mistaken.'

When Shorty stood up, he looked genuinely humble indeed.

'I'm sorry,' he said to Mandy Taylor, who hid her face in her hair.

'And to your brother. Go on.'

Knuckles sat up in his seat and beamed as Shorty mumbled something like an apology in his direction. 'Can I sit down now, Miss?' asked Shorty.

'No, not yet,' said Miss Quick.

She fetched a chair and put it beside her own desk.

'For the rest of the day, Noel, you will sit here—nice and close to me. Bring your books.'

As Shorty sat down in the seat beside the teacher, the rest of the class let out a cheer. It was the first time Shorty had ever been seen to blush.

CHAPTER TWO

SCONE WARS

Penny Brown and Mandy Taylor came out of school carrying a large biscuit tin each. It was a Wednesday, and Wednesday was cookery day for the girls of Miss Quick's class. Penny and Mandy had just baked dropped scones, and those scones were still warm and odorous within their respective tins.

Behind them, rather like a pack of wolves on the scent of something delicious, came Jimmy Zest, Gowso, Legweak, Knuckles and Shorty. The boys were hoping that the girls would offer them something from one of the tins. They knew it would not be easy. They knew it would be like getting blood out of a stone, but they were determined to have a go—especially Shorty, who was quite prepared to beg on all fours if need be.

He spoke first. 'Ah, go on, give us one of your scones.'

'No.'

'Please.'

'Go and get lost, Shorty.'

'Just one little one between us,' said Legweak. 'I'll let you see my locusts.'

Penny Brown almost stopped in her tracks. She wanted to inform Mr Legweak that of all the things in the world she wanted to see, the two pathetic locust prisoners up in his bedroom were last on her list. In fact, they weren't even on her list.

'Just ignore them, Penny,' advised Mandy Taylor, who had taken to shuffling along with very short steps. Nicholas Alexander was right behind her and she was afraid of being tripped up by that gorilla, who would then run away with her tin and eat every scone. Knuckles made Mandy very nervous.

'Aren't you forgetting something?' Jimmy Zest asked quietly. 'Isn't it better to give than to receive?'

These, of course, were not his own words. They were a cunning quotation from yesterday morning's Assembly. Penny Brown could not resist pointing out the truth.

'We were talking about the Third World, Zesty—not about you lot.'

'Just one!' cried Shorty, rather desperately.

'One miserable scone wouldn't break you—you must have fifty of them in that tin.'

Penny Brown came to a halt. She turned to face her tormentors, who had also come to a halt.

'Shorty. N-O spells No. When I give you one of these scones it will be the end of everything. The universe will shrink to a tiny dot and then the tiny dot'll disappear and there'll be nothing under the sun. In fact there won't be any sun. Absolute emptiness will take over. Right?'

A kind of absolute emptiness came over Shorty's face, for he hadn't a clue what Penny Brown was going on about. He turned instead to Mandy Taylor.

'And you needn't ask Mandy—*she* won't give you any, either, will you, Mandy?'

'I might,' said Mandy cleverly, 'if they came to school in their pyjamas.'

'Penny,' said Jimmy Zest in a rather soothing tone of voice, 'when it's the boys' turn to do cooking next term, we'll give *you* a share.'

'You couldn't boil water, Zesty.'

'Yes, I could.'

'I bet he can cook as well as you,' said Gowso loyally. Penny Brown regarded him with something like pity in her steady eyes. Such a statement proved once again that Gowso wasn't wired-up properly. Jimmy Zest might have a lot of information locked away in the computer he had for a brain, but when it came to cooking . . . well, Penny just knew she was better than he was.

And so did Mandy Taylor. 'Prove it, Zesty.'

'Prove what?'

'Prove that you can cook as well as Penny can. I dare you.'

'I can't. Not unless we have a cooking competition and have the results eaten by a tasting jury.

'So have a competition,' said Penny Brown hotly, 'and then we'll see, won't we? And I wouldn't give you one of these scones if you were monkeys at the zoo.'

The girls marched on down the hill, feeling good that they had cut one or two people down to their proper size. The boys, seeing that the cause was lost, made no effort to keep up with them. Shorty and Legweak hopped about the pavement scratching their armpits and grunting like a couple of escaped chimpanzees, while Jimmy Zest took Knuckles to one side and had a quiet word in his ear.

*   *   *

There had never been a chance that the boys would get a scone that afternoon. At eleven o'clock that Wednesday morning a picture of Penny Brown had mysteriously appeared on Miss Quick's chalkboard. The drawing consisted of a lot of squiggly lines near the bottom, while Penny herself was shown with a pigtail stuck up in the air—and there was a propeller on the end of the pigtail. Not a bow—a *propeller*. The implication was that she, Penny, was gently descending into a den of snakes.

They were all equally guilty, of course—Legweak had hidden the board rubber and the rest had laughed when she scrubbed the board with her sleeve and got her cardigan filthy. And four hours later they had the nerve to ask her for a dropped scone!

44

Mandy Taylor's scones were very well received at home. Her mummy gave them great praise and her daddy, who ate them with enormous knobs of butter, said they were ten times yummier than the ones you buy in the shops. No doubt he was exaggerating, thought Mandy, but still—she felt quite like a real cook. And it was important to be able to cook. As her friend Penny had pointed out the other day, good cooks would be more important after a nuclear war than professional footballers or fashion models or computer experts. These serious thoughts were interrupted by the telephone ringing in the hall.

'Mandy! It's for you. That boy Nicholas is on the phone.'

Good grief! What in the name of the stars above could Knuckles Alexander want to say to *her*? She shuffled unwillingly into the hall.

'Give yourself a shake, Mandy—the poor fellow's probably worried about his homework or something.'

Absolutely one hundred per cent totally wrong, Daddy. Nicholas

Alexander does not worry about things like homework and neither does his brother Shorty. Those twins do not know how to worry about anything. They are worry-free people whose purpose in life is to create problems for others to worry about.

So what *did* he want?

'Yes?'

'Is that you?'

No, Knuckles, I'm somebody else. 'What do you want?'

'You said that if we wear our pyjamas to school tomorrow you'll give us scones out of your tin, right?'

Mandy Taylor's mind became a blank for a second or two. School. Pyjamas. Scones. The three nouns did not seem to belong together in the same sentence.

'I didn't.'

'You did.'

'I did *not* say any such thing.'

'You did. Shorty heard you too. We'll be wearing our pyjamas tomorrow.'

'See if I care,' said Mandy, and set down the phone rather fiercely.

But she cared—oh, she *did* care. In

her mind's eye she saw them sitting in
class in their pyjamas, the first people
to do such a thing since schools were
first invented, and they would say that
Mandy Taylor put them up to it; she'd
dared them; she promised them a
scone if they would do it!

Mandy removed herself quickly to
her bedroom—the Taylors had several
phones—and called her friend Penny.

'Don't be stupid, Mandy. Nobody
would come to school in their pyjamas.'

'Well, they must be going to, Penny.'

'No way. Never.'

'Why then would they phone me and
ask a question like that if they're not
going to? I bet they were just getting
into bed when they remembered all of
a sudden what I said to them. Can't

47

you just see it?'

'But their mummy wouldn't let them!'

'There are mothers who can't cope, you know, Penny. There are *two* of them. Maybe the poor woman is worn out. I'm going to phone them back.'

'And say what?'

'I don't know. I'll say I'll give them a scone each if they don't wear their pyjamas.'

'That is a mistake, Mandy,' said a voice of steel.

'But I don't want to be involved.'

'That is exactly what the scroungers want you to do. It's a diabolical scheme, that's all it is, and I'll bet you anything you like that Jimmy Zest put them up to it. They're not to get so

much as a crumb, Mandy. OK? Promise?'

Reluctantly, Mandy gave her promise. No scones, no crumbs. Anyway, she reasoned, they would never do it—who would make themselves look ridiculous for the sake of a dropped scone? Penny was quite right, this was a time for sensible thinking.

'Problem sorted out then, Mandy?'

She gave a little start, and blushed slightly at her daddy's question as she came downstairs. 'Yes, thanks. Just a problem about homework.'

*   *   *

Thursday did not turn into a disaster until breaktime.

As a matter of fact, the morning began very well as far as Penny Brown and Mandy Taylor were concerned. Shorty and Knuckles turned up as usual in grey jumpers and trousers, which was a considerable relief. Then, after three or four problems involving fractional parts, and a spelling test,

Miss Quick wrote a sentence on the board and allowed an interesting discussion to happen. The sentence was: IF YOU KEEP A PET, YOU KEEP A PRISONER.

The debate was a fierce affair. In Penny Brown's opinion Jimmy Zest talked far too much and at one point practically accused Legweak of murdering his pet locusts. Legweak retorted that it was none of Jimmy Zest's business and declared, amid cheers, that he was saving up for a piranha fish as well.

All through the debate, though, Gowso kept stealing glances at Penny Brown like some secretive, sniggering know-all of a spy; and every time she caught Shorty's eye, he pointed at his chest and nodded madly as if someone was operating his head on invisible strings.

Something was cooking, there could be no doubt about it.

Then she saw that Knuckles Alexander had rolled one of his trouser legs right up to the knee. Underneath the trouser leg, neatly tucked into a black sock, was a maroon-coloured pyjama-leg.

Not so much as a flicker passed over Penny Brown's face as she turned away from the bizarre spectacle to confer with her friend Mandy—but Mandy was on her feet, speaking on behalf of pet lovers everywhere.

'You are forgetting something, Jimmy Zest. What about lonely old people? They keep pets, don't they? And where would they be if they didn't have dogs and budgies and things?'

Mandy sat down feeling quite pleased with herself. Nobody had thought of that idea, not even Jimmy Zest.

'Mandy. They're wearing their pyjamas,' whispered Penny.

'What?'

'*Under* their clothes.'

A single glance confirmed that this was the awful truth. Nicholas Alexander sat smiling all over his turnip of a face.

There was only time, before break, for a quick vote. Jimmy Zest lost the count by a show of twenty-seven hands

51

to five. Then the bell went and Miss Quick hurried off for her cup of coffee. The sound of her footsteps had scarcely died away before Knuckles and Shorty presented themselves at Mandy Taylor's table.

'Scones!'

'I do not know what you mean,' said Mandy weakly.

'Scones means scones, you don't need a dictionary to know what scones means,' said Knuckles. 'You said you'd give us scones if we wore our jammies to school and we're wearing them. See?' And he undid two buttons of his shirt in case further proof were needed.

'Me too,' said Shorty, with an eye on Mandy's purple plastic lunch box. It had a special compartment for a flask inside—Mandy's mother bought nothing but the best.

Mandy stared aghast at the smirking boys in front of her, and fiddled nervously with the gold ring on her little finger, for the horrible fact was that she had no scones with her. On the day when she needed them most, they were back home in their tin. She was about to offer the twins half a Mars bar each when Penny Brown spoke up at her elbow.

'What are you going on about, Nicholas Alexander?'

'She owes us scones.'

'What she owes you is a nice round zero, like that.' Penny made one with her thumb and finger to make sure he got the point.

'She dared us. We did it. Deliver!'

'Can't you recognize a joke when you hear one, you great twit? You're not getting a scone, and you're not getting anything else, either!'

It was a moment of incredible suspense. Gowso's eyebrows rose up and stayed up as if they'd been stitched there. Even the happy-go-lucky Legweak seemed unnaturally solemn. Was it possible that someone could call Knuckles a twit, and live? Something rough and physical seemed bound to happen in the crushing silence, for Knuckles was not a Jimmy Zest; he did not talk his way out of difficult situations.

Knuckles didn't even try. He just said, 'OK,' almost with a shrug of his shoulders, and walked to the classroom door with Mandy's purple lunch box in his hand. Shorty followed him through the door like a whippet, and they were gone.

*　　*　　*

The messenger who returned the lunch

box just before the end of break was Legweak. Mandy Taylor received it from him in silence, and turned it gently in her hands for signs of damage. There was a rather unsightly scratch near one of the hinges, but since Mandy could not put her hand on her heart and swear that this was a new scratch, she accepted for the moment that her property had not been abused.

However, the lunch box was not returned unopened. The Mars bar had gone. And the lovely big ripe pear. It was safe to assume that neither of them would ever be seen again.

'Right, Legweak! Who ate those things?' Penny Brown demanded to be told.

'You needn't blame me,' said Legweak. Mandy unscrewed the lid of her flask and found that her juice had been drained down to the last dribble. The fury of Penny Brown was such that for a few fleeting moments she wanted Knuckles and Shorty Alexander to be exterminated.

'You should tell Miss Quick the minute she comes in, Mandy. I'll back you up.'

'No.'

'But it's daylight robbery!'

'I know it's daylight robbery, but I did *say* it, Penny—I dared them to wear their pyjamas and they wore them. And if we tell Miss Quick they'll just show her their pyjamas and there'll be a whole fuss and we'll have to write out the school rules fifty thousand times. I just want to forget it, OK?'

No, it isn't OK, thought Penny. This was an example of Jimmy Zest and his cronies getting away with blue murder yet again. As far as she was concerned, she wanted justice, and she wanted apologies all round if she could possibly get them. But for the moment she let the matter pass.

CHAPTER THREE

EGG-SPLOSIONS!

The following week Penny Brown and Mandy Taylor were Litter Monitors. It was their job to remind people that empty crisp packets should be put in the wire baskets and not just dumped in any old place. On Friday, when they had almost finished their duty, Jimmy Zest appeared with a piece of plain white paper in his hand. Shorty and Legweak were with him, and those two did their best to keep their faces straight. But Penny Brown saw them smirking. She did not have to be the world's greatest detective to work out that they were up to something.

What could it be, she wondered?

'Could I have a word with you for a moment, Penelope?'

'What do you want, Zesty? You'd better hurry up, we're on litter duty.'

'It won't take long. I have drawn up a

list of rules for the match. They're on this piece of paper.' Jimmy Zest passed it over, saying, 'I hope you find them satisfactory.'

The page had been typed. Typical!

BROWN VERSUS ZEST

1. The cooked dish shall be plain omelette.
2. Each person shall provide his/her own eggs.
3. Each person shall provide his/her own frying pan.
4. Stephen Armstrong (also known as Legweak), Amanda Taylor and Nicholas Alexander (also known as Knuckles) shall be the tasting jury.
5. Each member of the tasting jury shall be blindfolded.
6. The venue shall be a neutral kitchen—to be decided.
7. The contest shall be held tomorrow morning at 0900 hours.
8. The winning omelette shall be the one that the majority

of the tasting jury likes
best.

Penny handed the list of rules to
Mandy so that she could goggle at
them, too.
'I hope you can cook omelettes,' said
Jimmy Zest.
'Certainly I can cook omelettes—
better than you can, Zesty.'
'You agree, then?'
'Where is it going to be?' asked
Mandy.
'We're working on that,' said
Legweak happily. 'We just want to
make sure that you don't chicken out
after we've made all the arrangements.'
'Right! I agree,' said Penny Brown.
'But I don't want Knuckles on the
tasting jury—Legweak and Mandy are
all right, but not him.'
The point of a Jimmy Zest pencil
passed through the offending name.
'And another thing, Zesty—the loser
buys Mandy a pear and a Mars bar.'
'Why?'
'Justice. Do you agree or not agree?'
After a look and a pause, Jimmy

59

Zest added the ninth rule to his list, and Shorty took the opportunity to shake Penny Brown's hand. 'May the best omelette win,' he said gravely.

Just for a second or two, some butterflies fluttered wildly in Penny Brown's tummy.

Of course, she was absolutely confident that she would win. Penny had cooked many omelettes for many people, including a whole tentful of Girl Guides—nobody had ever complained about her omelettes. But she wondered about Jimmy Zest. What a calamity it would be if, by some miraculous fluke, he managed to make a perfect omelette, and beat her! The news would be round the school like a flash and Knuckles Alexander would give the V for Victory sign with his fingers every time he met her.

'Don't be such a pessimist, Penny,' said Mandy when she heard these thoughts spoken out loud. 'I bet he's never cooked an omelette in his life!'

* * *

The hunt was on for Gowso.

Shorty and Legweak spent the best part of lunchtime looking all over the school for him, but to Shorty's amazement they couldn't find him anywhere. Shorty tended to regard Gowso as a kind of giraffe. As Jimmy Zest once pointed out, tall Gowso was one of those rare people who are more noticeable in a crowd than at any other time.

So where was he? They tried the computer room, the library and the music room. No Gowso. Legweak began to suspect that he had a secret life. Eventually they tracked him down to the tuck shop on the main corridor, where he sat like a miser among cardboard boxes of goodies, counting the tuck shop money for Miss Quick.

'We've been looking everywhere for you, Gowso,' said Legweak, as if Gowso had no business to be where he couldn't be found at the drop of a hat.

'No, you haven't,' said Gowso. 'You didn't look here or you would have found me.'

'We *have* found you,' Shorty pointed out.

'Well, what do you want?'

'A favour.'

'No.'

Gowso understood about favours. Usually they meant giving away something for nothing, or else a great deal of effort with no thanks at the end of it. People asked him for favours because they thought he was soft. He continued to construct £1 towers out of 5p coins.

'You haven't even heard what it is, yet,' Legweak pointed out.

Gowso counted on. He didn't want to hear, but Legweak let him know what the problem was, anyhow.

'You see, the thing is—we've set up this cooking competition between Zesty and Penny Brown tomorrow morning.'

'Saturday. And they're doing omelettes,' added Shorty.

'It's all fixed except for one thing. We haven't got a place for them to cook.'

'And what's that got to do with me?'

'Well, your kitchen's free on Saturday morning—isn't it?'

Gowso's arm gave an involuntary twitch and flattened two or three of his money towers. 'No. You're not using my house for a cooking competition.

'Ah, come on, Gowso, be a sport, it has to be a neutral kitchen.'

Shorty received a moody, Gowso stare. 'Let it be yours, then.'

'My mum's in. Everybody's mum is in on Saturday except yours. We'll make you one of the tasting jury—what about it, Gowso?'

'No!'

'Why not?'

There was no particular reason why not, just a thousand possibilities that a disaster would occur. They would wreck the place, break plates, explode something in the microwave, crack the new tiles, burn the house down— Gowso's panicking mind allowed him to visualize these happenings as if they were already ugly, incontrovertible facts. He swept the tuck shop money into a box and stood up.

'Use somebody else's kitchen,' he

declared while ripping open the store door. 'You must think I'm a nut case!' Then he zoomed down the corridor as fast as it was possible to travel without breaking into a run, which was Against the Rules.

*　　*　　*

On Friday afternoon Penny Brown and Mandy Taylor saw Jimmy Zest emerge from the supermarket carrying a flat, square package.

Penny seized Mandy's arm with a hand that felt like a talon. 'Do you see what he's got, Mandy?'

'Eggs.'

Besides a dozen eggs, Zesty was carrying a small, oval jar. Something about that jar made Penny Brown desperately suspicious. It looked like mustard, or maybe spices. Her heart gave a little flutter as if . . . well, as if Jimmy Zest knew more about cooking than she had bargained for.

He saw them coming. 'Hi.'

'Hi, yourself,' said Penny.

'I see you've got some eggs, Zesty,'

Mandy said. 'Going home to practise?'

'Yes. We have an electric frying pan with its own legs. I don't know whether to set the heat at 220 or 300. Heat is very important when you're doing eggs. I got a book out of the public library and it said that scrambled eggs continue to cook in the pot even if you turn the heat off.'

Flute! thought Penny. He's been doing *research*. 'What have you got in the jar?' she asked.

Jimmy Zest peered at the label. 'It says here "monosodium glutamate".' And away he went, nursing his eggs, leaving behind a rather startled Penny Brown. Monosodium glutamate, for heaven's sakes—what was *that*?

She knew Jimmy Zest so very well— this was exactly the kind of fancy trick he would try; he would slip something secret into his omelette and make it taste lovelier by far than her own.

She ran home, and was relieved to find her mother in the house.

'Mummy, have we got any monosodium glutamate in our cupboards?'

'Monosodium *what*?'

'*Glutamate*—have we got any?'

'No, what do you want it for?'

'To put in my competition omelette.'

Mrs Brown continued to water her half-dead spider plant. 'Penny, go away and give my head peace.'

By a quarter past nine on Saturday morning, Gowso was already a bundle of nerves.

There were seven people crammed into his kitchen—and it was not a big kitchen. And they were using Gowso plates, and Gowso knives and forks, and the cupboard doors were lying open, and right now Shorty had poked the upper part of his body into the Gowso fridge.

'What are you looking for in there, Shorty?'

'Nothing. I'm just seeing how cold it is.'

He had foreseen all of this, of course. If only his mother had not been a district nurse and on weekend call, none of it would be happening. Poor Gowso had said 'No', but he had the kind of friends who did not take 'No'

67

for an answer.

'Are you our mate or not, Gowso?'

'Yes.'

'No, you're not, or you'd lend us your kitchen.'

And so the emotional blackmail went on. He'd had to prove that his friendship was true by providing them with a neutral kitchen. He hadn't asked for any of this, he'd been forced into it by powerful personalities.

'Leave that cheese alone, Legweak!'

'Just a wee bit, Gowso. I'm starving.'

Legweak continued to nibble. As a member of the tasting jury he'd felt obliged to skip breakfast that morning.

Penny Brown and Mandy Taylor had set up their operation beside the electric cooker. As well as a non-stick frying pan and her eggs, Penny had a glass bowl and a plastic slice for turning eggs in a non-stick pan. An appalling moment occurred when she realized she had forgotten to bring along an egg-whisk—but Mandy opened two or three drawers and found that, sure enough, Gowso had one. Gowso saw this happening, and suffered.

In another corner, meanwhile, Jimmy Zest had plugged his electric frying pan into a socket normally reserved for the Gowso toaster, which had been shoved into the breadbin out of the way. Legweak, testing his blindfold, bashed into a spice rack on the wall and set a dozen little bottles trembling.

Gowso rushed forward to stop them falling. 'Look, stop rushing about, will you? There are seven people in this kitchen and this is not a *big kitchen.*'

'Ah, it's big enough, Gowso,' said Shorty, as if Gowso had nothing to be ashamed of.

With the frying pans now heating up nicely, the egg-breaking was about to begin. Penny cracked hers neatly on the rim of the glass bowl, and a yellow-eyed puddle formed at the bottom of the bowl without a trace of shell. It was a competent piece of egg-breaking and a very encouraging start.

Across the room, in the Jimmy Zest cap, Knuckles swung a wooden spoon at an egg as if he were a lumberjack tackling a redwood tree—and he

69

couldn't believe what happened. The egg did not break. The spoon bounced off it.

'Did you see that?' Knuckles addressed his question to the entire kitchen. 'That egg didn't break. And I gave it a real wallop. Hey, Zesty, that's some egg!'

'All eggs are tough,' said the knowledgeable Jimmy Zest. 'If you squeeze them in a certain way, you can't break them. Watch.'

He took the egg and carefully fitted each point of it between his palms so that for a moment he resembled a fortune-teller holding a rather tiny crystal ball. Then he pressed on the ends of the egg until his face turned bright red. Legweak took a step backwards in case he got a squirt of yolk up his nose, but the egg did not break.

'See? You try it.' He handed the egg to Knuckles. 'But you have to press on the points of the egg, not the middle.'

Knuckles tried it, and the egg did not break.

Nothing could prevent Shorty from

having a go next. He was so sure of his own strength that he donned Gowso's mother's apron so that he wouldn't get drowned in yellow squelch. An expression of agony transformed his face and his eyes became mere slits as he pressed and pressed. And the egg did not break.

'Jeepers!' said Gowso, who had momentarily forgotten his worries.

'It's hard-boiled,' said Legweak. 'Must be, Zesty.'

'It's not hard-boiled, it's to do with the internal construction of the egg. If you drop an egg from high enough up, it'll come down on its end and not smash.'

'Even from a helicopter?'

'Probably.'

Knuckles shook his head wisely. This defied common sense. 'Your head's a balloon, Zesty.'

'I'm telling you, it's the way hens make them.'

Legweak was curious. 'What about ducks?'

'Ducks can lay their eggs from twenty-thousand feet,' said Penny

Brown, raising her voice. 'Are you going to make an omelette, Jimmy Zest, or talk about ducks and hens and eggs all day? And another thing . . .' she waved Gowso's egg-whisk in his direction, '. . . all these are plain omelettes, we don't want anything fancy in them. Egg and only egg— right?'

She was referring to monosodium glutamate in all but name. Jimmy Zest nodded and broke an egg into his bowl. Legweak helped him to fish out some fragments of shell.

Penny was just about ready, now. Her yellow mix, thoroughly whisked in a little milk, waited only to be tipped into her pan. After a few moments more (she wasn't running the risk of her omelette getting cold by starting first) Mandy counted up to three, and officially said, 'Go!'

The omelettes slid into their respective pans with a soft hiss. Scarcely a sound could be heard in Gowso's neutral kitchen, and no one— not even Gowso himself—saw Knuckles, Shorty and Legweak make their exit through the back door.

Those three were heading for Gowso's garage. They had every intention of returning for the tasting of the omelettes, but in the meantime something had come up that required their urgent attention. It also required a ladder. They found one hanging on the garage wall. Knuckles supervised its removal without actually using his hands, for his pockets were full of eggs from Gowso's fridge.

The purpose of the ladder was to get Knuckles from the ground to the roof of the garage, where he walked up the slanting tiles like one born to the roofing trade. Once up there, he sat astride the ridge of tiles as a jockey might settle himself on a horse, and it didn't occur to him that if he fell he might easily break his neck.

An egg appeared in his hand.

'Right, Shorty, here goes. Super-egg.'

Knuckles stretched out an arm as straight as a flagpole. By opening his fingers the merest fraction, he allowed the super-egg to drop, and it landed at

Shorty's feet below with a quiet plop that quickly developed into an orange-coloured splurge on Gowso's cement.

'Told you,' said Legweak. 'Scrambled egg.'

Shorty gazed up at his brother with disappointed eyes. He had fully expected the egg to bounce.

'You weren't high enough up!'

'It can't be done, I'm telling you,' said Legweak. 'It's like hitting the thing with a hammer.'

'Shut up, Legweak,' snapped Knuckles, who was in no mood for pessimistic talk as he raised his eyes to Gowso's upstairs windows. 'That's where I should be—up there!'

The Alexander twins weren't beaten yet.

In the kitchen, meanwhile, Mandy Taylor was acting as a spy for Penny Brown. 'You should see Zesty's omelette,' she whispered. 'It's swimming in fat like an ugly yellow oil slick.'

'Has he sneaked anything into it?'

'Only salt. You should turn yours, Penny.'

Penny flipped her omelette. It was thick and light and fluffy, and deliciously browned. A quick glance across the room confirmed that Jimmy Zest's looked like a very good imitation of a pancake. It would take a miracle to get that thing ready for human consumption, she thought with satisfaction. Poor Mandy—she was going to have to taste it!

At that moment the Alexander twins passed through the kitchen as if one was towing the other. They did not pause to cast a sideways glance at either omelette, but sprinted up the stairs two at a time, bolted through a door and flung the window open wide like people possessed. They had lost their bearings on the way and were now in Gowso's parents' bedroom at the front of the house, a detail that did not concern them in the slightest.

Outside, and down below, Legweak watched in fascination as two upstairs windows flew open and an Alexander leg appeared through each. The twins sat astride the window sill, each with his arm outstretched, and each

with an egg
delicately   poised
between finger and
thumb for a
long drop. It
was like watching
some weird,
synchronized dance.

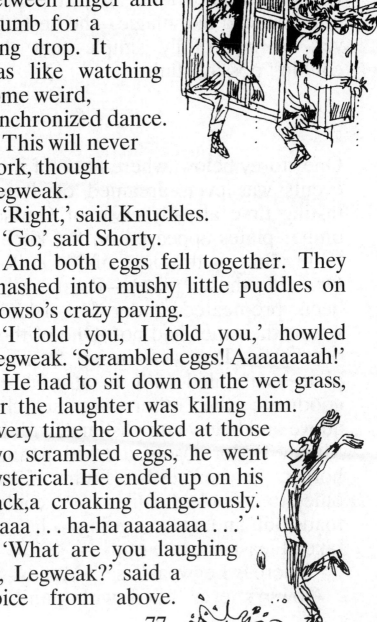

This will never
work, thought
Legweak.

'Right,' said Knuckles.

'Go,' said Shorty.

And both eggs fell together. They
smashed into mushy little puddles on
Gowso's crazy paving.

'I told you, I told you,' howled
Legweak. 'Scrambled eggs! Aaaaaaaah!'

He had to sit down on the wet grass,
for the laughter was killing him.
Every time he looked at those
two scrambled eggs, he went
hysterical. He ended up on his
back, a croaking dangerously.
'Aaaa . . . ha-ha aaaaaaaa . . .'

'What are you laughing
at, Legweak?' said a
voice   from   above.

77

'Cut it out or you'll get your head in your hand. Hey, wait a minute. Shorty! I've got another idea.' It just popped into his head like magic—the best idea yet; so beautifully simple that they couldn't possibly fail.

*   *   *

One storey below, where none of these events was even dreamed of, it was tasting time already. Two of Gowso's dinner plates appeared on the kitchen table along with some of his cutlery. One of those plates—Penny's—had been pre-heated under hot running water; the other had not. One of those omelettes—Penny's—sat up from the plate as if filled with an airy, golden goodness; the other was scorched above and below and glistened with fat. Mandy Taylor observed it with genuine horror in her eyes. Jimmy Zest's omelette looked like a cooked toadstool, and *she* was going to have to take at least one bite of it!

'Where *is* Legweak?' said Mandy.

Gowso's eyes filled with panic. If

Legweak was missing, what was he up to?

A slight delay now occurred while Penny Brown fetched the missing judge, whom she found writhing on the front grass like a poisoned worm. Then they had to wait some more while Legweak fitted his swimming goggles over his eyes. These goggles, when packed with kitchen roll, were his blindfold. Mandy simply tied a tea towel round her head.

Gowso finally became useful. He tossed a coin to decide which omelette should be tasted first. This business was conducted by sign language, since no words could be spoken in case the official tasters heard some kind of clue. Gowso pointed at Jimmy Zest—to indicate that he had won the toss; and Zesty pointed at Penny Brown—to indicate that he was putting her in to bat, so to speak.

Penny got ready to slide her omelette under the noses of the tasting jury.

'Are you sure you can't see through those goggles, Legweak?'

'I'm blind, I'm blind,' said Legweak.

'And do you faithfully promise to give a true opinion?'

'Certainly,' said Legweak.

After several wild prods with his knife, Legweak eventually struck omelette. Then he had trouble getting a piece on to his fork. Finally he missed his mouth with the fork and stabbed himself up the nose.

'Ow!'

'That is pathetic. You should be sitting in a high chair, Legweak,' Penny Brown informed him bluntly.

These were the last words spoken before the back door opened wide, and Mrs McGowan marched into her kitchen wearing her district nurse uniform. Poor old Gowso stared at his mother as if she were some kind of spook, and hot blood rushed to his face.

*   *   *

On that Saturday morning, when Mrs McGowan eased the bonnet of her car through her front gate, she noticed first of all that her bedroom windows were open, and her curtains flapping gently to and fro in a moderate breeze.

Even as she wondered how such an extraordinary thing could happen, her eyes took in other details—and these were every bit as extraordinary as her flapping curtains. There was a red-haired boy in her front garden, and he was about to throw a large, oval stone into the air. (She had no idea, then, that this stone was actually one of her own eggs.) As a matter of fact he threw it right over her roof—Mrs McGowan watched it rise, and pass between her chimneys, and disappear over the other side of the house, as a wild cry of 'WATCH OUT FOR THAT ONE, SHORTEEE!' broke about her ears.

She was about to get out of the car when another object, travelling in the opposite direction, fell out of the sky and landed on the windscreen of her nearly new Volkswagen golf.

She ducked, of course. The crack of the thing was tremendous. And when she looked up again, the albumen, the yolk and the shell of an egg were splattered across her windscreen.

With a palpitating heart, Mrs McGowan emerged from her car. That was when she noticed two more broken eggs on the crazy paving under her windows. That was when a second boy, identical to the first, appeared in her driveway with the speed of an Olympic sprinter. He held an egg on high. The boy was quite obviously delirious, for his eyes were lit up like two slits in a

Hallowe'en pumpkin. Apart from this, he was wearing her laminated pinny.

'Knuckles! It went smack on the ground and it didn't bust. I saw it! We got a super-egg, look. Missus, this is serious.' Shorty was not overawed by the uniform of a district nurse. 'It hit the ground, wallop, and just rolled over. Boy, I'm telling you, this here's some egg.'

Mrs McGowan concentrated her gaze, not upon the super-egg, but upon the two boys. 'Where did you get that egg?'

Knuckles didn't answer. Shorty, who was both honest and stupid, blurted out the truth. 'Out of Gowso's fridge.'

'I see. So it's my egg. Give it to me, please.'

At last it dawned on Shorty who she must be. 'But . . .'

'Give—it—to—me. *And* my apron, if you don't mind.'

The super-egg was delivered into the hands of its rightful owner.

On the way to her back door, Mrs McGowan could not fail to notice her ladder propped up against the garage and yet another broken egg. How many was that, she wondered as she entered her kitchen—three or four? And how many more?

Being a district nurse, Mrs McGowan was accustomed to dealing with little and large emergencies of all kinds. Even so, she closed her eyes briefly when she saw what was going on in her own kitchen. Things had been perfectly normal this morning when she left: now, the fridge door gaped open wide and she had no eggs left except the one in her hand; her utensils had been extensively used; a boy say at the table wearing swimming goggles; a girl had a tea towel round her head and really, all of a sudden, Mrs McGowan came to the end of her tether.

'I am dealing with lunatics,' she announced. 'You,' pointing at Gowso, 'up to your room. And close those upstairs windows while you're at it.'

Gowso seemed to glide through a crack in the door.

'The rest of you—out! I shall have something to say to your mother about this, Penelope Brown.'

'Please, Mrs McGowan,' pleaded Penny, 'couldn't we tidy up the kitchen first?'

Gowso's mother noticed her toaster in the breadbin and blinked. 'Yes, of course you can—by removing yourselves. Just pack up your pans, and *go*.'

As Jimmy Zest led the hasty retreat down Gowso's driveway, the handle of his four-legged frying pan stuck out from his armpit like a field-marshal's baton. After him, in swimming goggles, came Legweak, waving his fork. Mandy Taylor followed them meekly, for she was still in a state of shock. With her own eyes she had witnessed how the Alexander twins could disarrange a whole house in less time than it took to cook an omelette, and she was quite convinced that someone should put them in jail.

At the back of the group, Shorty was curious.

'Hey—who won the big omelette fight?' Penny Brown almost spoke up to claim victory, but decided instead to

let Jimmy Zest admit defeat.

He did no such thing. 'It was a draw.'

'A *draw*? What do you mean, Zesty? Your omelette was vile, it looked like a cooked banana skin. Ask Legweak, he tasted the thing.'

'Yeah,' said Legweak. 'It was rotten.'

'See? You owe Mandy a pear and a Mars bar.'

'All omelettes are rotten,' continued Legweak. 'I can't stand omelettes. Yours was rotten too.'

Penny Brown glared at Legweak for quite some time. There he stood with fork and goggles, ready and willing to judge between two omelettes when he couldn't stand omelettes, never ate omelettes, thought all omelettes were rotten. How could a person behave like that?

'Draw,' said Jimmy Zest.

So much for justice, thought Penny Brown.

The world was a place where people wore their pyjamas to school and nothing happened to them; where criminals could eat a person's pear in broad daylight and simply go free; where you could cook a bad omelette and get away with a draw.

'I am sick of you too, Knuckles Alexander,' she said all of a sudden. 'You mess up everything anybody tries to do.'

She might as well not have spoken. This personal attack was totally ignored by Knuckles, who borrowed a pencil from Jimmy Zest and was about to write the date on the egg he'd swiped back from Mrs McGowan's fridge.

'I'm going to keep this for ever,' he said, slipping the super-egg into his pocket.

'I bet it's broken by bedtime,' muttered Penny Brown as they turned into Mandy's drive.

dermist's shop in Monger's Lane.'
What!' said Penny Brown. 'Are you
gesting, Jimmy Zest, that we buy
a horrible dead thing?'
tuffed,' Jimmy Zest repeated
ly. 'There is a big difference
een being dead and being stuffed.'
ot if you're the squirrel,' Legweak
ted out.
andy Taylor said, 'Wise up, Zesty,'
crossed the room to comfort poor
Purvis, who was sitting with her
in a hanky.
next day, Saturday, Knuckles
is friends assembled early in the
ng in a quiet corner of Mercer's
for the funeral of his guinea pig.
ty carried a rusty shovel to dig
Knuckles had a green shoebox
his arm. Legweak surveyed the
rom the saddle of his bike and
who looked a bundle of nerves,
y with his long, black violin

Penny Brown and Mandy
vaited for Shorty to dig a hole,
passed on the latest
ion.

CHAPTER FOUR

GOODBYE, MISS QUICK

One Friday morning Miss Quick caught Shorty with a great glob of chewing gum in his mouth.

Really it was no wonder that she caught him, for Shorty practically showed it to her. He put his fingers in his mouth and pulled out a long, pink string as if his tonsils had melted. Then, 'Slurp-slurp-slurp', he gathered in the slack with his tongue.

Like magic, the wastepaper basket appeared under his chin.

'Spit.'

'Yes, Miss.'

'Thank you.'

Poor old Shorty had to listen to a lecture about classroom rules and why they should never be broken.

'I hope, Noel,' said Miss Quick, 'that you'll be on your best behaviour next term. I may as well tell you all here and now that I am leaving the school at the end of the term. I shall be very sad to go, but there it is. These things happen. You won't have me to teach you any more, you will have . . . someone else. Set out your English books, please.'

They were flabbergasted. Penny Brown cried, 'Flute!' and Shorty stood right up in his seat: 'Ah no, Miss.'

'I'm afraid so,' said Miss Quick.

At the back of the room Mavis Purvis, normally a quiet girl, looked ready to burst into tears.

'But . . . the holidays start at the end of next week,' she said.

'I am aware of that, Mavis. That's plenty of time for you to get used to the idea—I'm sure you'll like your new teacher very well. Get those books out, please, we have work to do.'

Breaktime arrived. When Miss Quick went for her coffee the class was curiously silent. Legweak opened a window and poked out his nose like a dog on the back seat of a car, and sniffed.

More bad news, this time from the canteen.

'Cabbage for dinner,' he announced.

90

'Legweak! How can yo[u] cabbage at a time like t[his]' Taylor inquired savagely.

Questions were poppin[g] like firecrackers. Why w[as] leaving? Where was she would their next teach she be awful, would sh would he be worse?

'Maybe,' suggested she's going to get marri

The practical Jimm the lid on his plas container.

'She'll have to be of course,' he pointe a pound each we something a little bi

It was a fine i received it with except for Knuckle bit miserable bec had just died.

Legweak sug umbrella, since it Miss Quick was n

'You can bu squirrels,' said J

tax
sug
her
'S
firm
betw
'N
poin
M
then
Mavi
nose
Th
and h
morni
Wood
Sho
with.
under
scene
Gowso
stood
case.
Whil
Taylor
Mandy
informa

'Have you heard about Mavis Purvis? She bought Miss Quick a crystal bell from the House of Glass, it's a really snobby shop—things in there cost a fortune.'

'Shhh,' whispered Penny.

The moment had arrived. Knuckles walked forward and placed the green shoebox into the tidy little grave. Then he turned to Jimmy Zest, who had thought up this funeral in the first place.

'That's it. Do we fill it up now, Zesty, or does Gowso play first?'

'Gowso plays first,' said Jimmy Zest with authority.

Gowso took out his fiddle. He was never very cheerful before a public performance of any sort, but on this special occasion he found himself more disconcerted than ever, for he had forgotten his music book.

'I only know two tunes without music,' he said mournfully.

The National Anthem was one of them, but it didn't seem suitable. The other tune wasn't much better, but it had to do. As Gowso played 'Happy Birthday to You' over the dead guinea pig, Mandy Taylor felt a terrifying fit of giggles coming over her. She gobbled her bottom lip to stop it moving. If Nicholas Alexander saw her even smile at the funeral of his guinea pig, he would murder her.

Penny Brown had a question. 'What was its name, Knuckles?'

'Dot.'

Knuckles stamped lightly on the grave where the guinea pig had been respectfully committed to the earth.

'She'll lie there for ever,' he said.

In actual fact Knuckles was wrong. Dot the guinea pig was dug up again on Tuesday.

*   *   *

On Monday morning Mavis Purvis presented Miss Quick with a beautiful crystal bell from the House of Glass. When Mavis started to sniffle, Miss Quick told her kindly not to be silly.

Then Billy Parks and Woggles walked to the front of the room with a monster of a parcel which turned out to be a rubber plant.

'We got it with our own money, Miss,' said Woggles.

Miss Quick thought it was the last word in rubber plants.

'I do hope,' she said, 'that no one spends all their precious pocket money on *me*.'

Jimmy Zest held an important meeting behind the bicycle shed at lunchtime.

'Listen,' he said. 'Miss Quick is leaving at the end of the week, you know. If we're going to get her a present you'll have to bring your money in tomorrow at the latest. So far

I've only got Gowso's pound.'

'Just one thing, Zesty,' warned Penny Brown. 'We don't want this money spent on a stuffed creature from the taxidermist's shop in Monger's Lane.'

Unexpectedly, Knuckles tackled Penny Brown with a question.

'What? What was the name of that shop—the taxi-something?'

'The taxidermist. He stuffs things, Knuckles.'

'What like?'

Penny Brown sighed. 'Look. If you catch a huge fish and you want it stuffed, you take it to a taxidermist and he stuffs it, right?'

'What with?'

'Knuckles. Do I look like an encyclopedia?'

Penny said impatiently. 'I don't know what with.'

In the meantime a good idea had occurred to Jimmy Zest.

'Tomorrow, when the money's all in, we'll go into town and have a look round the shops. We can buy a dictionary or something, Miss Quick loves big words. OK?'

Jimmy Zest counted hands. The verdict was unanimous.

*　　　*　　　*

It rained on the members of the Tuesday shopping expedition, but the weather had no effect on their determination to buy Miss Quick something really special so that she would remember them for the rest of her life.

Knuckles marched along the pavement with huge, enthusiastic strides. He had a zipped-up canvas bag in his hand. Gowso asked him what was in it.

'Fry your own fish, Gowso.'

'Huh,' said the offended Gowso, 'excuse me for breathing.'

They had reached the shops already. In the largest department store in town they considered bathroom scales, an adjustable spotlight, a golfing umbrella, and so many other things that Shorty gave up and went away to run up the down escalator and down the up one.

The problem was Mandy Taylor.

Each time they seemed about to agree on a suitable present, Mandy found something the matter with it.

'Hurry up and make up your mind, I'm warning you,' Jimmy Zest threatened darkly.

In a leather-goods shop, it was Legweak's turn to get bored. He slipped the strap of a handbag over his shoulder and walked round the floor like a swanky model at a fashion show. Knuckles laughed until he could only breathe in snorts. Shorty gave one of his piercing wolf whistles and the lady in charge came over in a temper.

She pointed to an untidy heap of handbags on the racks. Her hand was dripping with jewellery.

'Are you people buying or aren't you?' she said. 'Look at the pile of bags I have to tidy up, I suppose it doesn't occur to you that I have other customers to worry about. And what have you got in that bag? Open it up, please.'

Knuckles stared innocently at his canvas bag.

'What for?'

'You could easily have slipped something in there, I know how these gangs work.'

'Missus, it's only a dead body.'

'Open it up, please.'

So Knuckles pulled back the zip and lifted out a grubby green shoebox. Then he took the lid off the box and Gowso's eyes did a boggler. It was the same guinea pig whose funeral he had played at!

'That thing needs a vet,' said Legweak.

The skin wrinkled on the shop lady's nose. 'Get that disgusting beast out of here! All of you—get out of my shop immediately and don't come back!' And she bundled them on to the pavement so rudely that Mandy Taylor vowed never to allow her mother to open her purse in that shop again.

Knuckles explained why he had resurrected Dot. He said he was taking her to that shop Penny Brown had mentioned—the taxidermist—to see about getting her stuffed.

'Huh,' Gowso muttered, 'there wasn't much point in me playing at her funeral if you were just going to dig her up again.'

The premises of Jonathan Took, antique dealer and taxidermist, were situated at the far end of the historic street called Monger's Lane. Penny Brown, after one glance into the window, spoke one word: 'Flute!'

It was like magic in there. A squirrel sat on a branch, a badger peeped out of a hole, a crafty old fox buried his nose in a carpet of leaves. The owl on the highest branch seemed to be waiting only for night to fall before he would pounce on one of the furry little things at risk on the forest floor.

Knuckles took charge, since he was the only one with a dead body.

'Right, we're not all going in. Only Zesty and me and Dot.'

'This is a free country, Nicholas Alexander,' Penny Brown pointed out, and they all traipsed into the shop behind Knuckles.

An old-fashioned bell clanged above the door, and announced their arrival.

At first, Legweak complained that he couldn't see past his nose in that gloomy shop. A low roof kept the place extraordinarily dark, although a single shaft of light from the only window brightened the glittering glass eyes of small creatures all around. Legweak noticed the motionless forms of birds among the shadows of the highest shelves.

'Cuckoo! Cuckoo!' he called.

'This place,' said Gowso, 'would give you the willies.'

They didn't see the taxidermist, who was sitting in a corner so quietly that he might have been stuffed himself.

'State your business,' he said.

Jonathan Took was a tiny man in a leather apron. A quiff of grey hair stood up from his head like a spring and he wore a pair of half-moon specs on his bony nose. Knuckles produced his shoebox and set it on the counter.

'Mister. How much would it cost to have a body done?'

The taxidermist lifted Dot and held her in the light. His eyeballs swelled behind his thick lenses.

'Hm. A South American cavy. Related to the squirrel, the beaver and the rat. This animal has no commercial value.'

'Would you stuff her for me please, Mister? I want to keep her for ever.'

'I do not treat domestic pets.'

And so saying, Jonathan Took set Dot in the box and tapped his counter with two impatient fingers. Jimmy Zest wondered whether he had them insured, like surgeons.

'Kindly close the door after you when you go.'

Shorty wasn't ready to go just yet.

'Mister—did they ever stuff people?'

'There's a first time for everything,'

said Jonathan Took serenely.

'Shorty!' Penny Brown grabbed Shorty's arm and hauled him out of the shop.

The tradesmen of the town were putting up their shutters, and the rush-hour traffic jammed the streets outside. The shopping expedition was over, and still they had no present for Miss Quick.

'Quit moaning, Zesty,' said Penny Brown when Jimmy Zest complained. 'We didn't see the right thing, that's all.'

'You had your chance, Penelope,' said Jimmy Zest mysteriously. Then he ran ahead with Knuckles to bury Dot again before dark.

*   *   *

When Wednesday came and more presents arrived at school for Miss Quick it was sheer agony for those who hadn't bought anything yet.

'She'll think we don't care,' said the excitable Mandy Taylor. 'Only three more days and she'll be *gone.*'

103

At dinners, Penny and Mandy heard that two girls were saving up to buy a set of table mats for Miss Quick—and they came to a decision.

'Right,' said Penny, 'we'll ask Jimmy Zest for our money back and buy our own present. Those boys can buy what they like. Anyway they haven't a clue about proper shopping.'

But they couldn't find Jimmy Zest. As usual he proved to be invisible when there was money to be recovered. They met Shorty, who told them that Zesty had gone into town with Knuckles during lunchtime.

'What for?'

'Didn't ask,' said Shorty.

'Well you should have asked, Shorty. Jimmy Zest has every penny of our Miss Quick Fund in his pocket, did you ever think of that?'

Shorty hadn't thought of that. Nor was he particularly worried, for Jimmy Zest had pockets like Fort Knox. But Shorty was there with Legweak and Gowso when Penny Brown collared Jimmy Zest before he could escape from the classroom at the end of the school day.

'Zesty, we want our money back, Mandy and me. We're going to buy our own present. Two pounds, please.'

She held out her hand for the money, but nothing happened.

'Are you deaf, Zesty? We want our money.'

'You can't have it, Penelope. You had your chance to buy something yesterday and you took too long about it.'

Jimmy Zest nodded at Knuckles, who produced an evil-looking bird from his canvas bag, and handed it over. It had only one leg.

Jimmy Zest turned it upside down to read the inscription on the base.

'It says here *Gallinago*. That's Latin for snipe, I looked it up. It's got a leg missing, that's why it was cheap.'

Shorty stuck a midget gem sweet into the bird's long, delicate beak.

'That's some snout. Nearly as long as yours, Gowso. What's it for, Zesty?'

One person in the company knew exactly what this mangy, flea-bitten article was for.

'Are you stupid? You know perfectly well what it's for, he bought that thing, that . . . snipe . . . out of that creepy shop with our money. Other people buy crystal bells and perfume but not us. That . . . brute . . . is our goodbye present for Miss Quick and you wouldn't give it to your worst enemy, Jimmy Zest!'

This truth, as it slowly dawned, allowed them to see the one-legged snipe in a fresh and uncomplimentary light.

Mandy Taylor hated it. She could imagine a nice little note saying:

Dear Miss Quick, please accept this stuffed snipe from your grateful pupils.

Really, it was ridiculous.

None of them liked it. Legweak said it would scare Miss Quick's canary to death.

Knuckles, who had heard enough of their carping, returned the snipe to his canvas bag.

'Well hard luck. The money's been spent and that's what she's getting and that's that.'

'That's what you think, Nicholas Alexander,' said Penny Brown. 'We're in the majority. We'll sell it and buy a dictionary.'

'Listen,' said Knuckles, 'if you touch that snipe I'll bust your face. Come on, Zesty, let's go.'

Penny Brown stared after them, hot with fury. It was war.

*   *   *

The table mats were presented to Miss Quick the following morning and Miss Quick raved about them as if they were the last table mats in the world. Penny Brown and her allies were all nerves in case Jimmy Zest rose to his feet and handed over that despicable stuffed snipe.

Thank heavens, he didn't. Probably, thought Penny, he was saving it until her last day.

At breaktime Gowso came up with a genius idea. He said that the museum had rooms full of stuffed animals and probably they'd buy another one cheap if they could only get that snipe off Jimmy Zest.

But how were they to get it?

During lunchtime they spotted Jimmy Zest up the oak tree in the playground.

'Shorty,' said Penny Brown, 'go up there and tell him Miss Quick doesn't want that smelly bird, she's probably a vegetarian.'

'What's that?'

'Just tell him, Shorty.'

So Shorty climbed the oak tree, had a few words with Jimmy Zest, and climbed down again.

'He says is doesn't matter if she's a vegetarian, she's not going to eat it. He says she likes birds, she's got a canary.'

If people exploded, Penny Brown would have popped there and then. She ran to the bottom of the tree and yelled up through the branches.

'CANARIES ARE ALIVE, YOU SNOOK. THEY FLAP THEIR WINGS AND GO CHEEP-CHEEP.'

Mandy Taylor stepped forward with a threat.

'JIMMY ZEST. WE ARE GOING TO CALL AT YOUR MUM'S HOUSE AND ASK HER FOR IT.'

'You needn't bother,' said Jimmy Zest. 'It's not at my house and she'll not know what you're talking about.'

For once Jimmy Zest had let something slip. Gowso saw it at once.

'Knuckles must have it.'

Knuckles! Penny Brown spun round to question Shorty. 'Where would he hide it? You should know, Shorty, he's

109

your twin.'

'Certainly,' Shorty said without fuss. 'Never worry, I'll find it. He's got no secrets from me.'

It took them only five minutes to reach the back gate of Shorty's house after the end of school. Shorty lifted the latch and allowed Penny Brown, Gowso, Legweak and Mandy Taylor to tip-toe into his yard, which was almost empty except for an aluminium coal bunker and a guinea pig hutch. Shorty hurried inside to look under the bed and anywhere else that a stuffed snipe might be lurking.

He came back with bad news.

'No luck, he hasn't got it.'

'Oh, Shorty, are you sure?'

'I'm telling you, he's got no secrets from me.'

'Hey, look at what I've found,' said Legweak.

Legweak had discovered that the roof of Dot's hutch lifted right off—the stuffed snipe lay in a bed of fresh, dry straw, its glazed eyes staring up at them. Penny Brown grabbed the snipe, turned to dash out of the yard—and that's when she ran smack into Nicholas Alexander.

The astonished Knuckles glared at the guilty people in front of him, and it wasn't long before his temper began to rise.

'Put that back.'

'I will not. Our money bought it,' said Penny Brown. 'You and Zesty own two parts of it but we own five.'

Knuckles stepped forward and gave Penny Brown a hard push. So Shorty gallantly stepped forward, too, and shoved Knuckles against the yard wall. Then Knuckles punched Shorty, and Shorty punched Knuckles. One punch followed another, and soon the fists were flying.

Now that the yard door was lying open, Gowso made use of it. He was followed through by Mandy Taylor, Legweak, Penny Brown with the stuffed snipe, all of whom hared down the road in a high state of excitement—and they didn't stop until they had run all the way to Mrs Worthington's shop, where they dumped themselves on the public seat, and sat steaming.

They had to wait some minutes while Gowso got rid of the awful stitch in his side. This gave Shorty time to catch up with them. He looked a bit puffed round the face.

'Who won, Shorty?' asked Legweak, curious.

'We haven't finished yet,' said Shorty. 'It'll be a draw, though.'

They walked past the police station and the library until they came to the museum, which had an interesting revolving door. Shorty went round three times before completing his entrance and then looked about him as if he was ready, now, for the moving staircase.

'Get a grip, Shorty,' Gowso told him. 'They don't like messing about in here.'

An attendant in a peaked cap glanced at them and yawned. There was a sign above his head:

Please help. If you see anyone interfering with exhibits or removing them, inform an attendant immediately. All thieves will be prosecuted.

Gowso led the way to the rooms where the museum kept the stuffed animals. They had just passed a giant

112

elk with antlers as big as hat stands when a furious attendant suddenly appeared in front of Penny Brown.

'I don't believe this,' he said, 'I don't believe it! Under my very nose.' And he jabbed the buzzer on the wall with such power that he almost broke his finger.

At first, Penny Brown thought he must be crazy. Only when he snatched the snipe from her arms did she begin to realize what was happening.

Crafty Gowso knew already. He began to back out of the Nature Room.

Shorty said: 'But, Mister . . .'

'Be quiet, you thief. And *you!*'—the attendant meant Gowso—'if you leave this museum I'll send the police after you to your door, you just see if I don't.'

Except for an occasional twitch caused by fear, Gowso stood absolutely still.

Then a man in a grey suit arrived and bustled the five of them through a door into an office, and the first thing he said was, 'Do you people know how many years you can get for stealing an exhibit from a museum?'

Anyone who did not know the answer to that question need only to have looked at Mandy Taylor's face. Thousands of years.

The man pointed at Legweak, who swallowed.

'Names, please. You first.'

Legweak swallowed some more. He couldn't stop swallowing.

'Stephen Armstrong.'

'Penny Brown.'

'Mandy Taylor, sir.'

'Philip McGowan, sir.'

'Harry Irvine,' said Shorty, and Mandy Taylor gasped at the sheer nerve of him.

He wrote down their addresses, too. This quiet period gave Penny Brown time to do some thinking—everything had happened so quickly—and bravely, she spoke up.

'Sir, we didn't take it. That bird belongs to us. A boy called Jimmy Zest bought it. It was a present for our teacher.'

The gentleman in the official grey suit turned the snipe upside down.

'Look, do you see that mark? That is the mark of this museum, it is unmistakable.'

'But we only brought it in to sell it to you!' cried Mandy Taylor.

'Cheap,' added Shorty.

For the first time the official gentleman seemed a little doubtful. He spoke to Mandy Taylor.

'This Jimmy Zest—he was the one who got the snipe in the first place?'

'Yes, sir, he even knew its name in Latin.'

Down went Jimmy Zest's name and

address on the notepaper.

'I'm letting you go. But don't you people make any mistake about this, somebody's in trouble up to their neck and I know where you live. Run along.'

They took his advice. They ran out of the museum. Outside in the street Penny Brown had to jog to keep up with Gowso's big steps.

'I'm worried to death, you know,' she said frankly. 'What's going to happen to Zesty? Where did he get that snipe from?'

'From your man in Monger's Lane.'

'But *did* he, Legweak? We don't really know where he got it. Zesty didn't say. That museum person seemed awfully sure that the snipe was his. Maybe . . . Maybe he and Knuckles . . .'

'Stole it!' said Mandy Taylor.

Those were shocking words to hear. As they passed the police station, Gowso said mournfully, 'They'll take his fingerprints, you know.'

*　　　*　　　*

Legweak went for a spin on his bike after tea. When he saw the police car parked outside Jimmy Zest's house, he took his eyes off the road and ploughed straight into a privet hedge and fell to the ground in a heap.

Legweak, who loved his bike, didn't even take time to examine it for damage.

The police!

'They've come for Zesty!' he cried out loud. Within ten minutes they were all there. Gowso and Mandy Taylor, Penny Brown, Shorty and Legweak gathered across the road, aware that at any moment they might witness the arrest of Jimmy Zest.

The downstairs curtains were tightly drawn, so nothing could be seen of what was happening inside the house. Gowso, however, claimed to know.

'Behind those curtains,' he said impressively, 'Zesty is helping the police with their inquiries.'

'Give over, Gowso,' said Penny Brown. 'Oh, if only there was something we could *do*.'

But they could only wait.

Eventually the front door opened and Mr Zest stood on his step with two policemen.

'Here they come.'

'Flute, they're looking over at us.'

'They haven't got him, said Shorty. 'Zesty's not with them.'

This was true. The two policemen came down Jimmy Zest's drive without a prisoner. One of them called out distinctly: 'We'll pick him up in the morning, then.' Mr Zest shut his door and the policemen drove away.

Nobody knew what to make of these developments at all.

'In the morning?' said Penny Brown. 'Where are they going to take him in the morning?'

Gowso, who hadn't a clue what he was talking about, said, 'Maybe they've let him out on bail.'

*   *   *

On Friday morning, Miss Quick called through her roll of names for the final time. They answered 'Yes, Miss,' or 'Present, Miss' as usual and nobody was absent until she came to the last name of all.

'Jimmy Zest.'

Jimmy Zest hadn't missed a day at school for three years, so it was no wonder that Miss Quick seemed surprised to hear no reply.

'That's very odd,' she said. 'I wonder where he could be?'

Penny Brown wondered, too. She had worried about him for an hour at least before she had managed to get to sleep the previous night. Actually, she had repeated the whole story to her mum, who smiled when Penny mentioned the stuffed snipe. As if it was funny! 'Penny,' her mum said, 'close those eyes and go to sleep. Jimmy Zest is many, many things—but a thief he's not.'

'Pssst!' Penny heard Mandy hissing at her. 'Penny. Will I do it now?'

'OK, do it now.'

Mandy rose to her feet and smoothed down her skirt in a self-conscious way, as if aware that soon she would be the centre of attention, and she wasn't far wrong. Shorty and several other people came out of their seats to watch her hand over a small package to Miss Quick.

'Miss, Penny and I bought you this. It's really quite little but we hope you like it.'

It was a pocket dictionary. Miss Quick smiled and nodded, first at Mandy, then at Penny Brown.

'If you look inside it's got our names on it, Miss Quick. Penny and Mandy.'

Shorty, who had fidgeted all through this ceremony, could restrain himself no longer. He stood up again.

'Miss, I haven't got you a present.'

'That's all right, Noel. Really, it's all right.'

'Miss, some of us did get you a present but it didn't turn out right. We spent pounds, Knuckles and me brought in fifty pence each. Miss, it was a stuffed snipe but it was museum property and Zesty lost us all our money. Miss, I'm sorry I haven't got you a present.'

Great big unbelievable tears came into Shorty's eyes—and Miss Quick's watered too. Penny Brown bit her lip as she reached up her sleeve for a tissue. Gowso and some of the boys kept their heads down so that nobody could see if they were crying or not. It was dreadful. Mavis Purvis put her head on her table and just roared.

This display of emotion continued for half-a-minute or so, then Miss Quick sniffed and said, 'Right, that's enough of that. Mavis, stop that nonsense.' She turned to Shorty. 'Noel, did you say . . . a stuffed snipe?'

'Yes, Miss, it had a bigger beak than Gowso.'

Gowso complained bitterly that his beak was no bigger than anybody else's, and Miss Quick sighed.

There was suddenly a fearful and inexplicable scraping sound at the classroom door. When it banged open Jimmy Zest squeezed through, puffing and blowing and carrying a . . .

Well, nobody was very sure what he was carrying, actually. At first some people thought it was a tree, for it was evidently made of wood and seemed to have branches. However, they soon noticed that this thing had beautifully carved feet, and a curious hoop round the middle. It was twice as tall as Jimmy Zest and very, very difficult to manoeuvre through a classroom door.

Miss Quick said, 'In the name of glory . . . !'

Jimmy Zest paused for breath.

'Miss, Shorty and Gowso and Penny and Knuckles and Mandy and me bought you a present, it's a mahogany hatstand. You put your umbrellas in the hoop—see?—and your hats up there. It's Victorian. I could have got you buffalo antlers instead. Would you rather have had buffalo antlers?'

The astonished Miss Quick appeared to flounder in the torrent of words from Jimmy Zest.

'No. No, I wouldn't. I would rather have a . . . mahogany hatstand.'

'Miss, Miss,' shouted Shorty, 'didn't I tell you, didn't I tell you we had a present for you, Miss, have you got any mahogany hats?'

While Miss Quick walked round the hatstand to admire it from several different angles, Penny had a quiet word with the over-excited Shorty.

122

'Look, Shorty, the *stand* is mahogany, not the hats. You don't get mahogany hats.'

'Oh,' said Shorty.

Miss Quick made a short speech, in which she praised the mahogany hatstand as much as it was possible to praise anything, and said that she would probably have to buy a house with a Victorian hall to put it in. Also, she thanked them all for their presents and told them to work hard—that would be the biggest and best present they could give her. 'Oh dear,' she sighed. 'I'm going to miss you people very much.'

*   *   *

Knuckles, Penny, Mandy, Gowso, Shorty, Legweak and Zesty stood outside the school gates that afternoon to wave goodbye to Miss Quick in her little red car. Legweak said she'd probably buy a bigger one now that she'd won promotion.

The car disappeared over the brow of the school hill with the mahogany hatstand sticking out of the back.

'That's her gone for ever,' Knuckles said, in the same tone of voice he had used at his guinea pig's grave.

Penny Brown walked home from school with Jimmy Zest to ask him how he had managed to turn a stuffed snipe into a mahogany hatstand.

'It was that taxidermist, wasn't it? I knew he was evil the minute I set eyes on him.'

'Wrong again, Penelope,' said Jimmy Zest.

He hadn't bought the snipe in Jonathan Took's, but in the pawnshop across the road. Of course the pawnbroker said he hadn't known the snipe was stolen from the museum, but still, the policemen made him allow Zesty to choose another present for Miss Quick.

'That was this morning, Penelope. The policemen brought me and the present into school.'

'But why did you pick a mahogany hatstand, Zesty?'

'I liked it. It was unusual.'

So are you, Jimmy Zest, thought

Penny Brown. There was nobody like him in the world, he was unique. She also thought that this was probably just as well, for she couldn't bear it if there were two of him.